AN ADOPTION STORY
REVISED

The Mulberry Bird

By Anne Braff Brodzinsky, PhD
Illustrated by Diana L. Stanley

Perspectives Press
Indianapolis, IN

*T*he *Mulberry Bird* has been written with some consi-
deration for the natural habits of birds. However, it is
a fantasy, and therefore it is not intended to represent
the lives of real birds in any consistent way.

Perspectives Press
P.O. Box 90318
Indianapolis, IN 46290-0318

Printed in Canada
ISBN 0-944934-15-3

Library of Congress Cataloging-in-Publication Data

Brodzinsky, Anne Braff, 1940-
    The mulberry bird : an adoption story / by Anne Braff Brodzinsky;
illustrated by Diana L. Stanley. — Rev.
        p.   cm.
    Summary: Although she loves her baby very much, a young
mother bird chooses adoption because she is unable to give
him the home which he needs.
    ISBN 0-944934-15-3
    [1. Adoption — Fiction. 2. Birds — Fiction]
I. Stanley, Diana L., ill.   II. Title.
P27.B78616Mu   1996
[Fic] — dc20   95-2460
                                                               CIP
                                                               AC

For my daughter Shoshi

"If you become a tightrope walker and walk across the air," said the bunny, "I will become a little boy and run into a house."

"If you become a little boy and run into a house," said the mother bunny, "I will become your mother and catch you in my arms and hug you."

The Runaway Bunny by Margaret Wise Brown, Harper and Row, 1942

*T*his is the story of a mother bird who lived in a mulberry tree long ago. Although small and young, she was a strong little bird. Her short body feathers were grayish yellow; her longer wing feathers were marked with black and white.

In springtime, in the cool hours before sunrise, she loved to fly in great swooping patterns around the mulberry tree. Her special song could be heard through the singing of all the other birds.

> "Per-chic-o-ree,
> Per-chic-o-ree"

As the spring days grew longer, her body grew heavier, and she knew that it was time to prepare for a baby bird.

She built her nest of twigs and straw on the middle branches of the huge mulberry tree. Inside the nest, which was lined with soft feathers pulled from her body, she laid one lovely, pale blue egg. She knew that the baby bird inside the egg needed the heat of her body next to him in order to grow. She was pleased with the egg and admired it for a moment before lowering her warm breast into the nest to protect it.

When the right number of days had passed, she felt the egg move slightly. As she rose from the nest she heard a scratching sound from inside the egg. Soon the scratching became a tap-tap-tapping, and suddenly the shell cracked!

First the baby bird's beak appeared, then his sweet little pink-feathered body stretched the crack wider and wider, until finally he tumbled out, and the shell fell away.

He looked a little surprised at first, but soon began to chirp, hoping that his mother would know that he was hungry.

$\mathcal{M}$ other Bird flew in a circle around the mulberry tree, watching for enemies and looking for food. She brought only the fattest beetles and the juiciest berries to feed her baby. She screeched and flapped her wings furiously whenever unfriendly birds came too close to the nest. Taking care of a baby was a little harder than she had thought it would be.

She noticed that some of the other mothers had
father birds to help them. Her baby's father had
flown away long before she built her nest and laid
the pale blue egg. Mother Bird asked some other
birds she knew if they would help her take care of
her baby, but they were too busy taking care of their
own families.

Mother Bird began to realize that she would have
to take care of her baby alone, but she saw how
much he was counting on her and was determined
to do her best.

One morning, perched on her lookout branch,
Mother Bird sensed danger. It was not night-time,
but the sky slowly grew dark. The wind blew in
angry gusts against her feathers. Quickly she flew
back to the nest to prepare for a storm.

Carefully, she spread her wings over the nest and
covered her wonderful baby. Deep in her throat she
warbled, "Per-chic-o-ree, per-chic-o-ree" so that he
would not be afraid.

The storm was like others she had known. The
wind blew hard. The rain came pouring down. The
branches holding the nest swayed back and forth.
Usually birds can protect their nests and babies in
storms. Usually after the storm everything is all
right again.

But this time was different.

*H*igh in the mulberry tree was a dead branch
with no leaves or berries. In the wind the branch
broke away from the tree. As it fell, it caught on
the edge of the nest and pulled away a piece of
the carefully woven straw.

The baby bird was crouched in the corner of the
nest that was torn away. When that piece of the
nest fell, he fell, too. Fluttering his baby wings that
were not strong enough for flying and chirping
loudly, he disappeared quickly through the wet
leaves. As the rain poured down around her,
Mother Bird flew to the ground to look for him.

There were many broken branches and whirling
wet leaves under the tree, but before long Mother
Bird heard a soft crying sound, and there, next to
the tree trunk, was the little bird, trying to stand on
his tiny legs. Mother Bird fed him some beetles and
berries and tried to shelter him from the driving rain.

When the storm ended, Mother Bird had many problems. She wanted most of all to bring the baby back to the warmth and safety of his nest, but it would be many weeks before he could fly to the high branches where it rested. She knew she had to build a new nest for him, but she did not know how to build a nest on the ground. Each time she gathered the sticks and straw together, small gusts of wind or the baby's flapping wings would scatter them in all directions. When she left to hunt for food, she could not watch for the larger birds and forest animals who were a danger to the baby bird.

Mother Bird was afraid. She was younger than the other mother birds, and this was the first time she had had a baby to care for. In the evenings after the baby was asleep, she tried to think of ways to solve her problems. In the mornings she flew about frantically trying to build a nest on the ground, looking for food, and calling out warnings to enemies. She worked all day, every day and later and later into the nights.

*M*any days and nights went by, but the
problems did not go away. Again and again Mother
Bird tried to weave new twigs and straw into the
new nest, but it was not strong enough to hold the
growing baby bird. She tried to bring enough food
to him and keep him warm, but he was soon hungry
and crying again. Mother Bird was very sad. She
understood that a baby bird who did not have a
safe nest and did not have enough food to eat was
a baby bird in some danger. As she grew more and
more tired, she began to think that even though she
was doing everything she knew how to do, she
wasn't taking good enough care of her baby.

ad and confused, she went to see the wise
owl, who, it was said,could sometimes help to solve
problems that were too hard to solve alone. Mother
Bird cried as she told the owl about all the things
that had happened and all that she had tried to do.
She told him about being alone without any other
grown-ups to help. She told him about the storm
and how hard she was trying to make a nest strong
enough to hold her baby who had fallen. She told
Owl that her baby bird was on the ground and that
he was sometimes cold and hungry.

Owl listened quietly to everything that Mother Bird
said. He could see that Mother Bird loved her baby
very much, but when he thought about the broken
nest and the hungry baby bird he was worried. Owl
sat completely still for a long time. He was thinking
hard because the problem was hard. Finally, he said
softly and a little sadly, that he knew one way to
solve her problem, but it would mean that Mother
Bird would have to say goodbye to her baby bird.

M other Bird looked at the owl. She did not like what he had said. She did not want to say goodbye to her baby. Quietly though, she turned toward him as he began his story.

"Ever since the world began," said the owl, "there have been times when a mother has a baby she loves, but no matter how she tries, she cannot give him the things that he needs. When this happens, the mother sometimes looks for another family to love and take care of her baby".

Mother Bird was quiet so the owl went on. "There are bird families who have strong, safe nests with room for babies."

"There are mountain birds and city birds and seashore birds," said Owl. "You could think about the kind of family you would most want for your baby and I could help you to go and find them. You could listen to their songs and see what kind of nests they build. Then, if you thought they were a good family, we would take your little bird and fly with him to his new home. You would ask his new family to promise to share their lives with him and to care for him forever. They would adopt your baby and become his family".

*M*other Bird stood up suddenly, puffed out her
chest and shook all her feathers at Owl. "No!" she
said. "I will not let my baby go." Silently she flew
home alone.

She continued to try to protect and feed her little
bird. She circled the mulberry tree screeching and
flapping her wings when unfriendly birds came
too close. She fed him some fat beetles and all
the sweet berries she could find. She worked alone,
without stopping, hoping for a better answer than
the one that the owl had given her.

*J*ust as Mother Bird was starting to feel a little
more hopeful, she heard the deep rumbling of distant thunder and she knew another storm was coming. This storm was worse than the last one. The wind came tearing in, whipping branches in all directions and scattering Baby Bird's nest on the ground once again. Lightning darted like bright, crooked spears around the mulberry tree and the thunder was so loud it made the ground shake.

Mother Bird huddled over her baby bird as the fierce wind tore at her feathers and the cold rain poured down through the mulberry tree and soaked her body. She tried to sing to her baby, but the storm seemed to take her song away. She tried to comfort her baby, but her voice was like a whisper because she was afraid too. Mother Bird trembled, but she kept her wings spread over her baby bird. When the storm finally stopped, it took her a long time to feel strong enough to get back to taking care of Baby Bird. Finally she saw that he was very hungry so she drew herself up and wearily flew off to look for food.

When she returned, the baby was gone. She
searched for a long time among the fallen leaves
and broken twigs. She looked in the tall grass and
even underneath the thorny branches of a nearby
rose bush. Finally she found him. He was muddy
and shaking with cold. He could not eat the food
she had brought.

Mother Bird stood quietly for a few minutes looking
at her baby bird. Then she said softly to herself,
"I will go and bring back Owl."

*M*other Bird asked Owl to tell her what he
knew about mountain birds and city birds and
seashore birds. She wanted to know where they
found food, how they built their nests and what
kind of songs they sang.

"Mountain birds tuck their nests carefully into
crevices in the rocks," he said. "The mountains are
majestic, rising high into the sky, the air is cool and
there is plenty of food. Birds who live there believe
that they are part of the mountains' majesty and
they prefer it to all other places."

Watching Mother Bird carefully, Owl went on.

"Birds who grow up in the city become wonderful nest builders. They put their nests under rooftops, inside sculptures and deep in window wells. Finding food is exciting and challenging for city birds. Birds who live there believe that they are part of why the city 'hums' and they prefer it to all other places."

"What about the seashore?" said Mother Bird.

"Well," said Owl, "many shore birds weave their nests into grasses and roots on the ground. Their nests are deep and soft. Most find food at the edge of the water. Seashore birds call to each other over the waves in long vibrant songs. Birds who live by the seashore believe that they are part of why the air smells sweet and they prefer it to all other places."

*M*other Bird sat thinking for a long time.
Finally she said, "Someday, I will be older and
stronger. Someday, I will know how to be a mother,
but my baby cannot wait for me. My baby needs a
warm nest now. He needs protection from danger.
He needs family wings over him in storms."

Owl waited.

"Take us to the seashore," she said. "Help me find
a family for my baby who have built a strong nest
on the ground. Help me find parents who are ready
to help each other take care of a baby."

Owl and Mother Bird helped the tired wet baby into
the folds of Owl's warm wings.

All that day and all that night and for another day
and another night Owl and Mother Bird flew steadily
on. On the morning of the third day they reached
their destination–a lovely sandy beach on the coast.
The sea spray cooled them as they flew closer to the
grassy dunes.

*F*ar below on the beach two birds had built a
strong nest in the grass. They had waited for a
baby for a long time. They hoped a mother bird
who needed a family for her baby would find them
and choose them to take care of her baby.

Some mornings they looked westward out over
the dunes. Maybe she would come to them from
behind the soft roll of the sea grass.

Other mornings they stretched their necks toward
the sky. Maybe she would come to them out of the
wide blueness or from behind a fluffy cloud. Each
day as they waited, they added more of their softest
feathers to the inside of the nest.

One brilliant, sunny morning, high above the waves,
they saw two birds flying toward them. They saw
that one of them was Owl. The shore birds knew
that Owl sometimes helped mother birds who
needed families for their babies. As Mother Bird
and Owl flew closer, the shore birds saw that Owl
was carrying a baby in his wings. He was bringing
a baby who needed a home.

T he shore birds could not wait until Owl, Mother
Bird and the baby reached the beach, so they flew
up over the waves to meet them. Mother Bird heard
them calling out to her and she knew the call was
a song of welcome and of love. As the shore birds
dipped their wings to invite Mother Bird and Owl to
land in the grass near their home, Mother Bird saw
how strong and graceful they were.

When Mother Bird, Owl and Baby Bird had landed
safely on the beach, Mother Bird stepped out ahead
of them to stand with the shore birds. She saw that
their nest was large and beautifully made. Supple
twigs and dried seaweed were woven evenly to
form the walls and she could see that the base of
the nest was fastened securely to the roots of the
sea grass which grew around it. Inside, the nest
was lined with many layers of downy gray feathers.

The shore birds stood close beside Mother Bird and
promised that they would love Baby Bird and hold
him safely in their family.

*M*other Bird's heart was pounding as she heard their promises. She looked at them standing proudly by their beautiful nest and imagined her baby sleeping in those downy feathers. She knew then that they were the right family to take care of her baby.

When Baby Bird was safely in his new home, Owl flew swiftly out over the waves. Before following Owl, Mother Bird flew to the mast of a nearby sailboat and watched her baby's new family circle around him.

"How safe he will be," she thought, "and warm and dry."

"All grown-ups have one problem that stands out above all the others," she thought. "Saying goodbye to my baby is mine." Then taking a deep breath for courage, she flew high into the sky, higher than she had ever flown before, and, swooping widely in her favorite patterns, she sang...

"Per-chic-o-ree, per-chic-o-ree," to say goodbye.

*B*aby Bird was too young to remember all that had happened. But Mother Bird was not. She would always remember.

Mother Bird loved Baby Bird all of her life. She remembered the day that he was born and the smell of his sweet baby feathers. Her memories were mixed with sad and happy feelings. She was sad that she had to say goodbye, and could not help her baby grow up. Over the years, though, she learned that he was becoming strong and fine, just as she was, and that made her happy.

That little bird who had been born in a mulberry tree grew up happily on the beach. His parents told him about his birthmother and the story of the storms and the broken nest. They also told him how hard she had tried to build a new nest and to give him the things that he needed. He learned about Owl and the long journey from the mulberry tree to the seashore. He learned that coming to live with his new family was called being adopted.

Most of the time when he thought about being adopted, he was happy. Sometimes though, when he was alone, he felt sad. He thought about his birthmother. He tried to imagine her living in the mulberry tree and he wondered if she ever missed him.

Other times he felt confused and angry about being adopted. On his confused days he wished his feathers looked more like his family's feathers. He also wondered how any storm could be bad enough to make his birthmother choose another family for him, and he wished he could ask her why she had not kept him with her in the mulberry tree.

H is parents helped him when he was sad or angry or confused. They knew it was hard for him to understand why he had been adopted and that trying to figure it out was something he had to do.

As he grew he learned to know the call of sea birds, to catch the brightest silver minnows in the foam, and to build a strong and secret nest of grass and down. His parents taught him how to avoid danger and to solve problems by himself. They taught him new songs and took him to his favorite places in the dunes. In winter, the family flew with other birds to warmer places, and when spring came, they returned to their beach to build new nests.

He loved the rhythm of their lives together, and,
as the years went by, he came to feel stronger
and more sure of himself.

Being adopted, he decided, was having two
families—one far away but not forgotten, and
one that greeted him each morning, surrounding
him with the flutter of their warm feathered bodies
and the noisy chorus of their singing.

nne Braff Brodzinsky's interest in adoption is multifaceted. Herself an adoptive parent, Anne was also part of the Rutgers research team which produced the definitive study on what children think and understand about adoption at various ages and stages of intellectual development. Her doctoral research centered on issues of how birthmothers cope with grief. Dr. Brodzinsky is a psychologist in private practice in South Orange, New Jersey.

Diana L. Stanley is a free lance artist working from Fort Wayne, Indiana. A graduate of Indiana-Purdue University at Fort Wayne's Department of Fine Arts, her previous book illustrations include *Perspectives on a Grafted Tree* and the 1986 black and white version of *The Mulberry Bird*.

 Perspectives Press
Post Office Box 90318
Indianapolis, IN 46290-0318

Since 1982 Perspectives Press has focused exclusively on infertility, adoption, and related reproductive health and child welfare issues. Our purpose is to promote understanding of these issues and to educate and sensitize those personally experiencing these life situations, professionals who work in these fields and the public at large. Our titles are never duplicative or competitive with material already available through other publishers. We seek to find and fill only niches which are empty.

Please write Perspectives Press for a complete catalog.